MOTHER GOOSE'S NURSERY RHYMES

HUMPTY DUMPTY
AND OTHER FAVORITES

ILLUSTRATED BY
ALLEN ATKINSON

AN ARIEL BOOK

BANTAM BOOKS
TORONTO • NEW YORK • LONDON • SYDNEY • AUCKLAND

HUMPTY DUMPTY AND OTHER FAVORITES
A Bantam Book
April 1985

Art Direction: Armand Eisen and Tom Durwood

ISBN 0-553-15340-4

Published simultaneously in the United States and Canada

Printing and binding by
Printer, industria gráfica S.A.   Provenza, 388   Barcelona
Depósito legal B. 335-1985
PRINTED IN SPAIN
0 9 8 7 6 5 4 3 2 1

"No, no, my melodies will never die,
While nurses sing or babies cry."
                    —Mother Goose

HUMPTY DUMPTY sat on a wall,
Humpty Dumpty had a great fall.
All the king's horses and all the king's men,
Couldn't put Humpty together again.

THIS LITTLE PIGGY went to market,

This little piggy stayed home;

This little piggy had roast beef,

MOTHER GOOSE'S NURSERY RHYMES

This little piggy had none;

And this little piggy cried
Wee!
Wee!
Wee!
all the way home.

JACK SPRAT could eat no fat,
His wife could eat no lean;
And so, betwixt them both, you see,
They licked the platter clean.

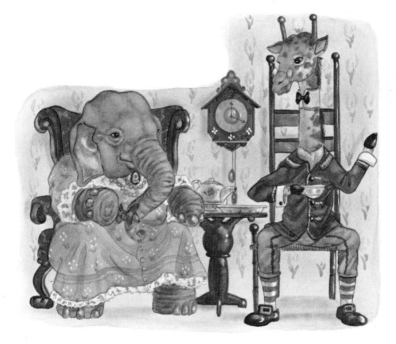

RUB-A-dub-dub,
Three men in a tub,
And who do you think they be?
The butcher, the baker,
The candlestick maker,
Turn 'em out, knaves all three!

THERE WAS an old woman
who lived in a shoe,
She had so many children
she didn't know what to do;
She gave them some broth
without any bread;
She scolded them soundly
and put them to bed.

TERENCE McDIDDLER
The three-stringed fiddler,
Can charm, if you please,
The fish from the seas.

ONE, TWO, buckle my shoe;
Three, four, open the door;
Five, six, pick up sticks;
Seven, eight, lay them straight;
Nine, ten, a big fat hen;
Eleven, twelve, I hope you're well;
Thirteen, fourteen, draw the curtain;
Fifteen, sixteen, maids in the kitchen;
Seventeen, eighteen, maids in waiting;
Nineteen, twenty, my stomach's empty.
Please, ma'am, to give me some dinner.

PEASE PORRIDGE HOT
Pease porridge cold,
Pease porridge in the pot
Nine days old.
Some like it hot,
Some like it cold,
Some like it in the pot
Nine days old.

HOT CROSS BUNS!
Hot cross buns!
One a penny, two a penny,
Hot cross buns!
If your daughters do not like them
Give them to your sons,
But if you haven't any of these pretty little elves
You cannot do better than eat them yourselves.

BIRDS OF A FEATHER flock together,
And so will pigs and swine;
Rats and mice will have their choice,
And so will I have mine.

ONE, TWO, three, four, five, six, seven,
All good children go to heaven,
Some fly east, some fly west,
Some fly over the cuckoo's nest.

THREE LITTLE kittens they lost their mittens,
And they began to cry,
Oh, mother dear, we sadly fear
That we have lost our mittens.
What! lost your mittens, you naughty kittens!
Then you shall have no pie.
Mee-ow, mee-ow, mee-ow.
No, you shall have no pie.

MOTHER GOOSE'S NURSERY RHYMES

The three little kittens they found their mittens,
And they began to cry,
Oh, mother dear, see here, see here,
For we have found our mittens.
Put on your mittens, you silly kittens,
And you shall have some pie.
Purr-r, purr-r, purr-r,
Oh, let us have some pie.

The three little kittens put on their mittens,
And soon ate up the pie;
Oh, mother dear, we greatly fear
That we have soiled our mittens.
What! soiled your mittens, you naughty kittens!
Then they began to sigh.

MOTHER GOOSE'S NURSERY RHYMES

OH, THE BRAVE old Duke of York,
He had ten thousand men;
He marched them up to the top of the hill,
And he marched them down again.
And when they were up, they were up,
And when they were down, they were down,
And when they were only halfway up,
They were neither up nor down.

HICKUP, hickup, go away!
Come again another day;
Hickup, hickup, when I bake,
I'll give to you a butter-cake.

45

HIGGLEDY, PIGGLEDY, my black hen,
She lays eggs for gentlemen;
Gentlemen come every day
To see what my black hen doth lay.
Sometimes nine and sometimes ten,
Higgledy, piggledy, my black hen.

THREE BLIND MICE, three blind mice,
See how they run! See how they run!
They all ran after the farmer's wife,
Who cut off their tails with a carving knife.
Did you ever see such a sight in your life,
As three blind mice?

MOTHER GOOSE'S NURSERY RHYMES

THERE WAS an old woman tossed in a basket
Seventeen times as high as the moon;
But where she was going no mortal could tell,
For under her arm she carried a broom.
Old woman, old woman, old woman, said I!
Whither, oh whither, oh whither so high?
To sweep the cobwebs from the sky,
And I'll be with you by and by.

MONDAY'S CHILD is fair of face,

Tuesday's child is full of grace,

Wednesday's child is full of woe,

Thursday's child has far to go,

Friday's child is loving and giving,

Saturday's child works hard for his living,

And the child that is born on the Sabbath day
Is bonny and blithe, and good and gay.

MOTHER GOOSE'S NURSERY RHYMES

HUSH-A-BYE BABY

On the tree top,
When the wind blows
The cradle will rock;
When the bough breaks
The cradle will fall;
Down will come baby,
Cradle and all.

ABOUT THE ILLUSTRATOR

Allen Atkinson is one of America's most beloved illustrators, whose works include *The Tale of Peter Rabbit* and other tales by Beatrix Potter, *The Velveteen Rabbit,* and *Mother Goose's Nursery Rhymes,* among others. Mr. Atkinson lives in rural Connecticut, where he was born and raised. His favorite subjects for his paintings are the well-known children's stories which he read as a child. In addition to book illustrations he enjoys creating toys for children.

Allen Atkinson has designed four charming stuffed bean-bag toys: Humpty Dumpty, Little Miss Muffet, Simple Simon, and a mouse from Three Blind Mice, all based on his artwork in *Mother Goose's Nursery Rhymes.* For information, write to The Toy Works, Box 48, Middle Falls, N.Y. 12848.